The Totally Terrifying Three

For John, who always gets me with his diagonals - H.O.

For my Totally Terrifying Three: Tanja, Monika and Luka - D.M.

First published in 2011 by Hodder Children's Books

Text copyright © Hiawyn Oram 2011
Illustration copyright © David Melling 2011

Hodder Children's Books, 338 Euston Road, London, NW1 3BH
Hodder Children's Books Australia, Level 17/207 Kent Street, Sydney, NSW 2000

The right of Hiawyn Oram to be identified as the author and David Melling
as the illustrator of this Work has been asserted by them in
accordance with the Copyright, Designs and Patents Act 1988.

A catalogue record of this book is available from the British Library.

ISBN: 978 1 444 90302 7

Printed in China

Hodder Children's Books is a division of Hachette Children's Books,
an Hachette UK Company

www.hachette.co.uk

The Totally Terrifying Three

Hiawyn Oram
and
David Melling

Hodder
Children's
Books

A division of Hachette Children's Books

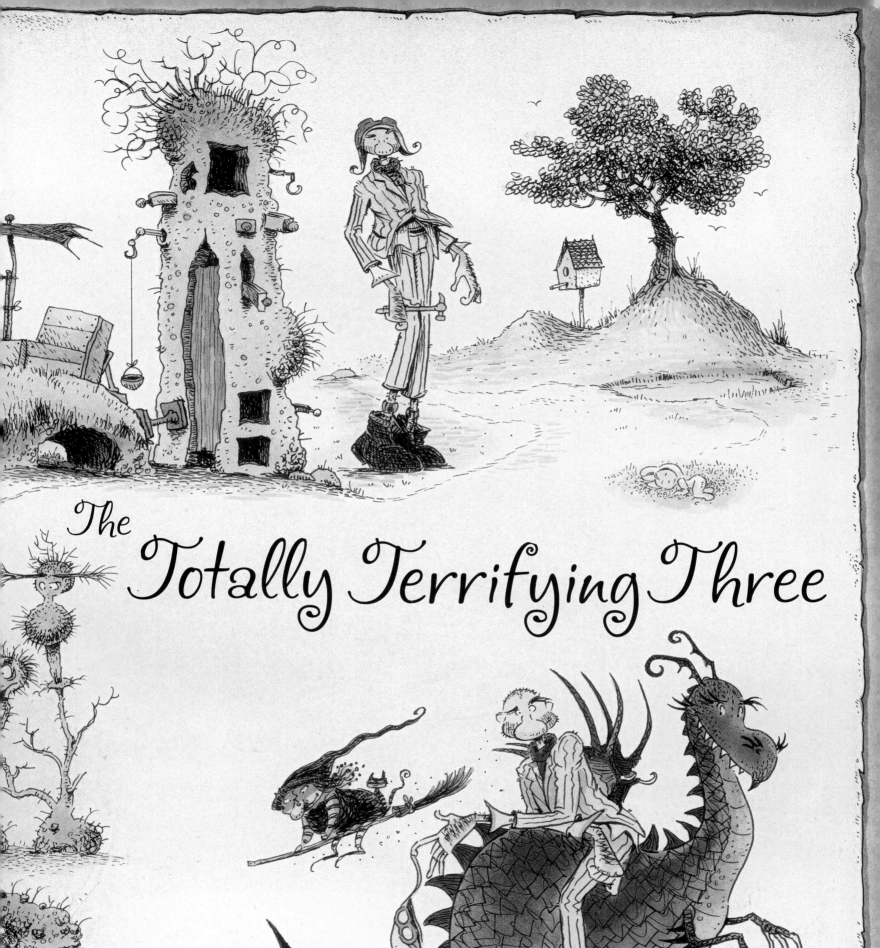

The Totally Terrifying Three

Once there was a Dragon
who was convinced he was

TOTALLY TERRIFYING.

One look at himself in the mirror and

he nearly jumped out of his skin.

"TOTALLY TERRIFYING DRAGON ALERT!"

he'd shout before he went anywhere which only made everyone dash, dive or RUN for their lives.

One day he said to his little pet Wiggles, "We're out of here. I can't keep on like this, frightening my neighbours out of their wits."

Wiggles raised his eyes to the skies but he helped the Dragon pack and off they set.

It wasn't long before they came upon a Witch
scaring herself silly in her magic mirror.

"TOTALLY TERRIFYING WITCH ALERT!"

she screeched as soon as she saw them.
"Don't look at me if you want
to keep your socks on!"

"Hold on a moment," said the Dragon.
"I'm the frightening one around here.
At the sight of me, giants' knees knock
and mountains turn to jelly."

"Well, you don't scare me," said the Witch.
"I don't?" said the Dragon.
"In that case we should go along together."

So they went along together and they
hadn't gone far before they came upon
a Giant terrifying himself in
his mini car mirror.

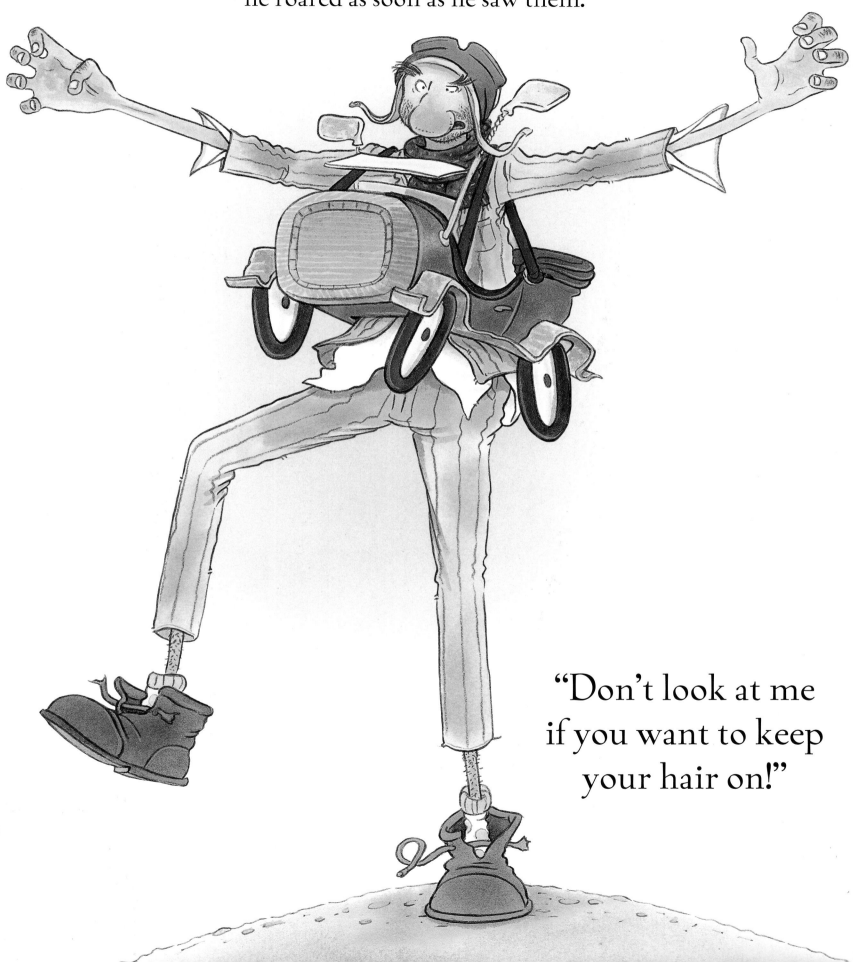

"Hang on a tiddly tad," said the Dragon,
"we're the scary ones in the neighbourhood.
We scare the pants off people and the spots off the spotted ones."

"Well, you don't scare me,"
said the Giant.

"We don't?" said the Dragon.
"In that case we should go along
together."

So they went along together and they hadn't gone far
before they stopped for a picnic and came
upon a Toddler.

Her name was Not-So-Tiddly and she
didn't say a lot but whatever she
said made sense.

"Nice Giant, nice Giant," she cooed. "Give me a ride on your shoulders
so I can see what I can't see from toddling."

Well, no one ever called that Giant nice if they knew what was good
for them, but a Toddler is a Toddler so he gave her a ride on his shoulders.

And when he put her down, she toddled over to the Witch and gurgled, "Sweet Witch, sweet Witch, give me a fly on your broomstick so I can know what I can't know from toddling."

Well, no one called that Witch sweet if they wanted to see another birthday, but a Toddler is a Toddler so she gave her a fly on her broomstick.

And when the Witch brought her down, Not-So-Tiddly
toddled over to the Dragon and babbled,
"Dear Dragon, dear Dragon, sing me a sweet song, a lullaby,
so I can dream what I can't dream while toddling."

At once, the Dragon settled her in his arms and sang
her the only lullaby he knew.

And when she was fast asleep he tiptoed over
and gently laid her down in the buttercups.

Then he strode back to the others and said,
"Well, here's the thing. We don't scare
each other, and we don't scare
Not-So-Tiddly, so who do we scare?"

"Take a new look," barked Wiggles.

And now when they looked, they saw themselves as
they'd been with Not-So-Tiddly...

...and nearly jumped out of their skins in surprise.

"I'm certainly silly," said the Witch, "but not one bit scary."

"I'm generally jowly," said the Giant, "but gi-normously jolly."

"And I'm an itsy on the ugly side, but totally UNterrifying," said the Dragon.

"Why, like this, we could go along forever scaring absolutely NOBODY!"

And when we last heard, that's just what they were doing –
going around together with a sign that said:

Although once in a while and strictly for the fun of it they still enjoyed...

...scaring the socks off
THEMSELVES!